B.L. 4.0

# A Spoon for Every Bite

## for Every

### Una Cuchara Para Cada Bocado Bite

By **Joe Hayes**
Illustrated by **Rebecca Leer**
CINCO PUNTOS PRESS · EL PASO

# A Spoon for Every Bite

## Una Cuchara Para Cada Bocado

A long time ago there lived a couple who were so poor they owned only two spoons— one for the husband and one for the wife.

Hace mucho tiempo había un matrimonio que era tan pobre que nomás tenía dos cucharas, una para la mujer y otra para el marido.

Their neighbor was very rich.
His big house was filled with fine
furniture, and he was very proud
of his wealth and his possessions.

Su vecino era muy rico. Su casona
estaba llena de muebles finos. El rico
estaba muy orgulloso de sus bienes y
sus posesiones.

One year the poor couple had a baby, and the wife said to her husband, "Why don't we ask our neighbor to be godfather to our child?"

"But he's rich and we're poor," the man protested. "Why would he want to be our *compadre?*"

"You never know," said the wife. "He might accept."

So the poor man spoke to their neighbor, and the rich man did accept. They took the baby to be baptized, and the neighbors became *compadres.*

Un año los pobres tuvieron un bebé, y la mujer le dijo al marido: —¿Por qué no le pides al vecino que bautice a nuestro hijo?

—Pero él es rico y nosotros somos pobres —protestó el hombre—. ¿Cómo va a querer ser nuestro compadre?

—Tú no sabes —dijo la esposa—. Es posible que acepte.

Así que el pobre se lo pidió al vecino y éste aceptó. Llevaron al nene y lo bautizaron, y los vecinos se hicieron compadres.

One day the poor woman said to her husband, "Now that our neighbor is our *compadre,* we should invite him to eat supper with us this evening."

"How can we do that?" the man asked. "We have only two spoons."

So they didn't invite the rich man that day. They saved their pennies and bought a third spoon. Then the poor man invited his *compadre* to come for dinner.

Un día la señora pobre le dijo a su marido:
—Ya que el vecino es nuestro compadre, debemos invitarlo a cenar esta noche.

—Pero, ¿cómo? —preguntó el hombre—. Sólo tenemos dos cucharas.

Así que no invitaron al rico ese día. Guardaron sus centavitos y compraron una tercera cuchara. Luego el pobre convidó al compadre rico a cenar.

The poor woman made a delicious soup, and when the men arrived she led the rich man to the place with the shiny new spoon. "Sit here, *compadre*," she said. "You get to use our new third spoon."

The rich man could scarcely believe his ears. "Do you mean to say you own only three spoons?" he asked.

"Until this morning we had only two," the poor man told him. "We bought a new one so that you could join us for dinner."

La señora pobre preparó un caldo sabroso, y cuando los hombres llegaron, condujo al rico al lugar donde lucía la nueva cuchara: —Siéntese aquí, compadre —le dijo—. Usted puede usar nuestra nueva cuchara.

El rico apenas podía creer lo que oía. Preguntó:—¿Quiere decir que ustedes no tienen más de tres cucharas?

—Hasta esta mañana nomás teníamos dos —le dijo el pobre—. Compramos otra para que usted pudiera cenar con nosotros.

The rich man laughed aloud. "You had only two spoons! And you bought a third one for me to eat with! Why, I have so many spoons I could use a different one each day of the year if I wished to."

El rico soltó una risa:
—Ustedes tenían solamente dos cucharas. ¡Y compraron otra para mí! Pues yo tengo tantas cucharas que podría usar una distinta cada día del año, si se me antoja.

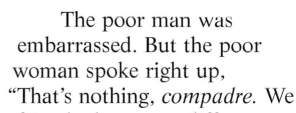

The poor man was embarrassed. But the poor woman spoke right up, "That's nothing, *compadre*. We have a friend who uses a different spoon for every bite he eats."

The rich man shook his head, but the poor man knew what his wife meant. "It's true," he said. "Our friend uses a different spoon for every single bite he eats."

The rich man was so upset by the idea that someone might live even more lavishly than he did that he couldn't enjoy his soup.

Al pobre le dio pena. Pero la mujer replicó:
—Eso no es nada, compadre. Nosotros tenemos un amigo que usa una nueva cuchara para cada bocado que se come.

El rico movió la cabeza, pero el pobre entendió lo que su mujer estaba diciendo.

—Es cierto —dijo—. Nuestro amigo usa otra cuchara para cada bocado que se come.

Al rico le disgustó tanto la idea de que alguien llevara una vida aún más extravagante que la suya que no pudo disfrutar del caldo.

That night he lay awake thinking about it.

Pasó la noche despierto, pensando en ello.

The next day the rich man's servant came running to the poor man's house. "What did you give my master to eat last night?" he demanded.

"He ate the same thing we did—the tastiest soup my wife has ever made."

"Your soup must have driven him crazy. This morning at breakfast he insisted on using a different spoon for every bite he ate. After one bite with a spoon, he ordered me to get rid of it."

The poor *compadre* smiled to himself. "And what does your master tell you to do with the discarded spoons?"

"He told me, 'Give them to my *compadres*. They have only three spoons.'"

Al otro día el sirviente del rico llegó corriendo a la casa del pobre. Gritó: —¿Qué le dieron de comer a mi amo anoche?

—Comió lo mismo que nosotros, el mejor caldo que mi mujer ha preparado en su vida.

—El caldo de seguro lo volvió loco. Esta mañana, cuando desayunó, insistió en usar una cuchara distinta para cada bocado. Comía un bocado con una cuchara, luego me ordenaba botarla.

El compadre pobre se sonrió entre sí. —Y ¿qué le dice su amo que haga con las cucharas desechadas?

—Me dijo "Regálalas a mis compadres. Ellos nomás tienen tres cucharas".

At lunch and at dinner the rich man did the same thing. That night the servant left a pile of spoons beside the door of the poor couple's house. The next day the rich man kept asking for a new spoon for every bite. After one week the servant informed him there were no more spoons in the house.

"Get me some more," the rich man growled. "Do you think I'm too poor to buy spoons?"

The servant bought all the spoons in town, and then he had to travel to other towns to buy spoons.

En el almuerzo y la cena el rico hizo lo mismo. Aquella noche el sirviente dejó un montoncito de cucharas junto a la puerta de la casa de los pobres. Al día siguiente el rico siguió pidiendo otra cuchara para cada bocado. Al cabo de una semana el sirviente le dijo que ya no había cucharas en la casa.

El rico gruñó: —Cómprame más. ¿Me crees tan pobre que no puedo comprar cucharas?

El sirviente compró todas las cucharas en el pueblo, y luego tuvo que viajar a otros pueblos para comprar más.

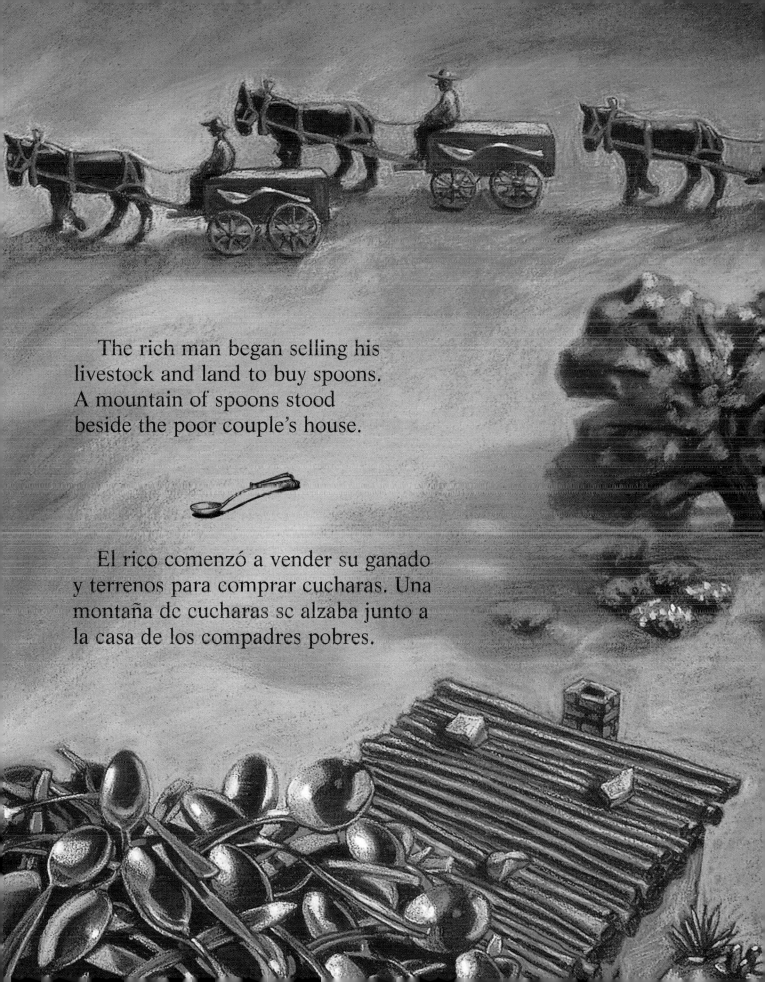

The rich man began selling his
livestock and land to buy spoons.
A mountain of spoons stood
beside the poor couple's house.

El rico comenzó a vender su ganado
y terrenos para comprar cucharas. Una
montaña de cucharas se alzaba junto a
la casa de los compadres pobres.

In a year the rich man squandered all his wealth. And there were just three spoons in his house. He walked angrily to the poor couple's house and pounded on the door.

"You lied to me!" he roared at them. "No one can use a new spoon for every bite. I have proved it. I was the richest man around, and not even I could do that."

Dentro de un año el rico despilfarró todo su caudal. Y quedaron solamente tres cucharas en su casa. Caminó enojado a la casa de los pobres y golpeó la puerta.

—Me mintieron —les bramó—. Nadie puede usar una cuchara para cada bocado. Lo he comprobado. Yo era el hombre más rico de estas partes, y ni siquiera yo podía hacer eso.

"You're mistaken, *compadre,*" the poor man said. "Day in and day out, year in and year out, our friend uses a different spoon for every bite he eats."

"Take me to meet this friend," the rich man demanded.

The poor couple took their rich *compadre* to the nearby Indian pueblo. They went to their friend's house. The Indian and his wife welcomed the *compadres* and invited them to stay and eat a meal.

"That's just what I came for," the rich man said. "I want to see you use a new spoon for every bite you eat."

—Está equivocado, compadre —le dijo el pobre—. Día tras día, año tras año, nuestro amigo usa una cuchara distinta para cada bocado que come.

—Llévenme a conocer a ese amigo suyo —insistió el rico.

Los pobres llevaron al rico al pueblo indio que estaba cerca. Fueron a la casa de su amigo. El indio y su mujer les dieron la bienvenida a los compadres y los invitaron a entrar para comer.

—Es justamente por eso que he venido —dijo el rico—. Quiero verte usar una cuchara distinta para cada bocado que comes.

"Spoon?" asked the Indian. "This is the only spoon I use." He pointed to a stack of tortillas on the table. He broke off a piece of tortilla and scooped up some beans. The beans and the spoon disappeared into his mouth.

"He'll never use that spoon again," laughed the poor man.

Again the rich man was too upset to eat his meal. He got up from the table and walked home sadly.

—¿Cuchara? —le preguntó el indio—. Ésta es la única cuchara que uso.

Señaló una ración de tortillas en la mesa. Rompió una tortilla y con el pedazo tomó unos frijoles. Los frijoles y la cuchara desaparecieron dentro de su boca.

—No vuelve a usar esa cuchara —rio el pobre.

Otra vez, el rico estaba demasiado alterado para comer. Se levantó y caminó cabizbajo a su casa.

But the poor couple enjoyed every bite their friends served them—spoon and all. And then they walked home smiling. They knew that when they had sold all the spoons their rich *compadre* had thrown away, they would live the rest of their days in comfort.

Pero los pobres aprovecharon cada bocado que les sirvieron sus amigos, con todo y cuchara. Luego caminaron sonrientes a casa. Sabían que cuando hubieran vendido las cucharas que el compadre rico desechó, pasarían el resto de la vida sin necesidades.

# A NOTE FOR READERS AND STORYTELLERS

In telling this story, I have combined two elements of the Hispanic story tradition of the Southwest. The deceptive reference to the use of a tortilla as an eating utensil is cast in the form of a picaresque tale featuring two *compadres,* one poor but clever and the other rich and overbearing.

Several brief tales and *chistes* hinge on the tortilla as a spoon that is used only once. From a high school teacher I heard a Mexican version in which a proud *conquistador* brags to a humble Indian that his king eats off plates of silver and gold. Feigning indifference, the Indian replies that his chief is so rich he uses a different spoon for every bite. In an Anglo-American variant, a seasoned traveler on the Santa Fe Trail yarns a greenhorn about the high style of life in New Mexico with the same idea. The joke is well-known to the old ones in New Mexico. On one occasion as I told my version at *El Rancho de las Golondrinas* Historical Museum south of Santa Fe, I noticed an elderly Hispanic gentleman in the group turn toward his wife when I said the phrase "a spoon for every bite" and silently mouth the word *tortilla.*

Humorous tales about rich and poor *compadres* abound in Hispanic story lore. In his compendious collection of Spanish narrative in the Southwest, *Cuentos españoles de Colorado y Nuevo Mêjico,* Juan B. Rael dedicates an entire section to *los dos compadres*, and many stories that are otherwise categorized involve two individuals identified as *compadres—el uno rico, el otro muy pobre.* In one such tale, the tortilla/spoon joke is briefly repeated.

Curiously, while the old tales so often portray an almost adversarial relationship between *compadres,* the actual relationship is quite the opposite. The role of godparent is highly esteemed, and parents typically choose a very dear friend to fill it. The tales of *los dos compadres,* however, are quite old and perhaps reflect the time when the wealthy *hacendado* would serve as godfather to all the children born to his *peones* as an expression of noblesse oblige. Whatever the true reason may be, these tales serve as a reminder that folktales cannot always be viewed as accurate expressions of the contemporary mores and practices of the culture from which they derive.

FIRST EDITION 10 9 8 7 6 5 4 3 2 1
Library of Congress Cataloging-in-Publication Data

Hayes, Joe. [Spoon for every bite. Spanish & English] Spoon for every bite = Una cuchara para cada bocado / by Joe Hayes; illustrations by Rebecca Leer.— 1st ed. p. cm. Summary: In this folktale from New Mexico, a rich man tries to prove his wealth by using a new spoon for every bite and in the process is served a pretty dish of comeuppance. ISBN 0-938317-93-8 (alk. paper) [1. Folklore—Southwest, New. 2. Folklore—Latin America. 3. Spanish language materials—Bilingual.] I. Title: Una cuchara para cada bocado. II. Leer, Rebecca, ill. III. Title.
  PZ74.1.H37 2005
  398.2'0979'02—dc22

2004029757

**Cover and book design by Paco Casas**